MW01028449

This book belongs to:

The Friendship Garden

Disney's Out & About With Pooh
A Grow and Learn Library

Published by Advance Publishers
© 1996 Disney Enterprises, Inc.
Based on the Pooh stories by A. A. Milne © The Pooh Properties Trust.
All rights reserved. Printed in the United States.
No part of this book may be reproduced or copied in any form
without written permission from the copyright owner.

Written by Rita Balducci
Illustrated by Arkadia Illustration Ltd.
Designed by Vickey Bolling
Produced by Bumpy Slide Books

ISBN:1-885222-57-2
10 9 8 7 6 5 4 3 2 1

It was early morning. Bright rays of sunshine were streaming through Winnie the Pooh's window.

"Ho-hum!" Pooh yawned, blinking and stretching in his snuggly nightshirt. "What a sunshiny day! I think I'll celebrate by having a little smackerel of honey for breakfast."

"Goodness!" Pooh exclaimed, opening his eyes wide. "What has happened to all my honey?" His cupboard shelves were empty from top to bottom.

Pooh noticed the dabs of honey on his nightshirt.

Then he remembered getting up to quiet a rumbly tummy in the middle of the night.

Suddenly a loud buzzing noise caught his attention.

"Buzzzz, buzzzz, buzzzz," went the noise. Pooh looked
up and saw a tiny bee flying above his head.
  "Hmmmm," Pooh said, watching the bee carefully.
"Where there are bees, there's honey. I think I'll follow that

bee right back to his hive." But just as Pooh spoke, the bee
darted away.

 "Wait for me!" Pooh shouted, forgetting that he was still
in his nightshirt.

Pooh ran as fast as his little round legs could carry
him. He ran all the way to Rabbit's garden, where the bee
disappeared into the dark center of a very tall yellow flower.
Pooh leaned way back to see where the bee had gone

and fell — KERPLOP! — right into Rabbit's cabbages.

"Who's there?" called Rabbit, rushing over.

"It's me — Pooh," Pooh said, brushing dirt off his nightshirt. "I was just following a bee to find some honey, but he hid up there in that funny yellow tree."

Rabbit looked up. "That's not a tree, Pooh," he said. "It's a sunflower."

"A sunflower?" Pooh said. "What a wonderful thing! That must be why it's so bright and warm here in your garden!"

"No, no, Pooh," Rabbit said. "Sunflowers are called that because they turn their heads toward the sun. See how they are all facing the same way?"

Pooh nodded. "What smart flowers," he murmured thoughtfully.

Rabbit was very proud of his sunflowers. "Now, Pooh,"
he continued, "if you like, I will give you some sunflower seeds.
Then you can grow some sunflowers of your very own!"

Pooh thought this was a splendid idea, and took the packet of black and white seeds.

"Oh, thank you, Rabbit!" Pooh called as he left the garden. "I'm sorry I fell on your cabbages!"

Pooh was very excited about having his own garden.
"I must tell Piglet!" he thought. And clutching the
seeds in one paw, he knocked on Piglet's door.
"Good morning, Pooh," Piglet said. "Won't you join me
for breakfast?"

Pooh gratefully accepted Piglet's offer. Between gulps
of honey, he explained about the sunflower garden he was
going to plant. "They are flowers of Very Great Brains," Pooh
said solemnly.

"A garden is a lot of work," Piglet told Pooh. "I'll get my shovel and help you."

"I'll keep the seeds in here with the honey," Pooh said
to himself, dropping them into the sticky jar that Piglet had
given him. "That way I won't lose them."

Piglet tried to explain to Pooh about weeds and watering. "Now, Pooh," Piglet began, "it's very important to...Pooh?" Piglet looked around.

There was his friend, stretched out in the sun and snoring away.

"I'll just start digging," Piglet decided. "Pooh can plant the seeds himself when he wakes up."

Shovel up, shovel down. Up, down, down, up. Piglet moved stones and dug up the ground in the hot sunshine.

"I think it's time to plant the seeds, Pooh," he finally called to his friend.

But Pooh just smiled and rolled over. "Thank you, Piglet," he said without opening his eyes. "I'll plant them as soon as I wake up."

Piglet shrugged. "Never mind, Pooh," he said. "I'll be back to help you again tomorrow."

The next day when Piglet arrived at Pooh's garden,
Pooh was already outside, licking honey from his paws.
"Are you ready to plant the seeds, Pooh?" Piglet asked.
Pooh mumbled something from inside the honey jar,

then sat back and looked back at Piglet gratefully.

"You're very kind to help me, Piglet," Pooh said. "Growing a garden is very hard work, you know." And with that Pooh licked his lips and began to sing.

Dig and water,
Weed and wait;
Hurry up, flowers!
Don't be late!
Turn to the east,
Turn to the west.
Facing the sun
Is what you like best!

Pooh liked his song so much that he decided to sing it again. Piglet knelt down and poked a stick into the dirt, making holes for the sunflower seeds.

Just then Roo came hopping by.

"Hello, Roo," said Pooh. "I'm going to plant my sunflower seeds today."

"Don't forget to pat the dirt down when you're done," Roo reminded him.

Days passed. Piglet and Roo showed up faithfully every morning to help Pooh in his garden. Watering, weeding, patting, pulling — working in the garden *was* hard work. Pooh did his part by adding new words to his song every day.

"Nothing's happening," said Roo, peering closely at the ground.

"Gardens take time," Piglet said, crouching to get a closer look.

"Would anyone like some honey?" sang Pooh.

The next day, Rabbit happened by.

"We've dug and watered and weeded," Piglet sighed. "But still no sunflowers."

Rabbit scratched his head. "That's very odd! How deep did you plant the seeds?"

Piglet and Roo turned to Pooh.

"Seeds?" Pooh said slowly.

Pooh peered into the honey pot. "Uh-oh," he said in a sad voice.

Then he pulled out one tiny sunflower seed dripping with honey.

"Gardening makes me hungry," Pooh tried to explain. "I thought the sunflower seeds would help keep my strength up."

For a moment, no one knew what to say. Then Rabbit cleared his throat.

"Well, now, that's all right, Pooh," he began. "I think I can help. Come with me." And so the three friends followed Rabbit to his garden, where lots of sunflowers were standing straight and tall.

Rabbit handed out shovels and pointed to the ground.
"Each of you, dig a deep circle around a sunflower," he
instructed them. "And make sure you don't hit any roots."

Piglet and Roo started right in. Pooh leaned on his
shovel to watch.

"You too, Pooh," called Rabbit. "Dig in!"

Pooh, Piglet, Roo, and Rabbit each dug up a sunflower. They carefully carried the flowers back to Pooh's garden and planted them there.

"Well, Pooh, how do you like your garden now?" asked Rabbit.

"It's *our* garden," said Pooh. "Because without all of you, I wouldn't have a garden at all!"

"Pooh," said Piglet as the four settled down for a rest, "shouldn't we give our garden a name?"

"Oh, yes," Pooh nodded. "What a good idea!"

Everyone thought and thought. Finally Pooh said, "What about naming it the Friendship Garden?"

And from that day on, that's exactly what their garden was called.